Elephant Small
and the splashy bath

Sally Grindley • Andy Ellis

little ORCHARD

this

little  ORCHARD

book belongs to

....

....

For Claire, Mike, Olivia, Max and Tom

AE

ORCHARD BOOKS
96 Leonard Street, London EC2A 4RH
Orchard Books Australia
14 Mars Road, Lane Cove, NSW 2066
1 86039 500 7 (hardback)
1 86039 746 8 (paperback)
First published in Great Britain in 1998
Copyright text © Sally Grindley 1998
Copyright illustrations © Andy Ellis 1998
The right of Sally Grindley to be identified as the author and Andy Ellis
as the illustrator of this work has been asserted by them in accordance
with the Copyright, Designs and Patents Act, 1988.
A CIP catalogue record for this book is available from the British Library.
Printed in Italy

Elephant Small was grubby.

"I'll run you a bath," said Elephant Mum.

"But I don't want a bath," grumbled Elephant Small.

"You need a bath," said Elephant Mum.

Elephant Mum felt the water with her trunk. "Just right," she said.

"But I'm scared of the water," wailed Elephant Small.

"Bathtime is fun," said Elephant Mum. "Hold onto my trunk and I'll lower you in."

"Don't let me fall!" squealed Elephant Small as the water rose up round his tummy.

"I'm all wet," whimpered Elephant Small. "I want to get out."

"Perhaps you'd like some bubbles?" said Elephant Mum and she tipped something green into the water.

"Now, splash with your trunk,
Elephant Small," said
Elephant Mum.
SPLASH! he went.

SPLISH ! SPLOSH! SPLASH!
SPLASHY! SPLASH!
Bubbles flew into the air.
"OOOH!" giggled
Elephant Small.

Elephant Small blew bubbles round the bathroom while Elephant Mum scrubbed him clean.

Then he lowered his trunk into the water and sucked. . .

"What *are* you doing,
Elephant Small?" asked
Elephant Mum.

WHOOOOOSH!
Elephant Small blew the water
out all over Elephant Mum!
"OOOOH!" he giggled.

"Time to get out I think,"
said Elephant Mum.

"When can I have a bath again?"
laughed Elephant Small.
"Bathtime is fun!"